This book was written using the power of the imagination of a young mind.

To Eben I hope you like my first ever book
Lots of love
Dilly

This is Bella. Bella loves school and loves to play her violin.

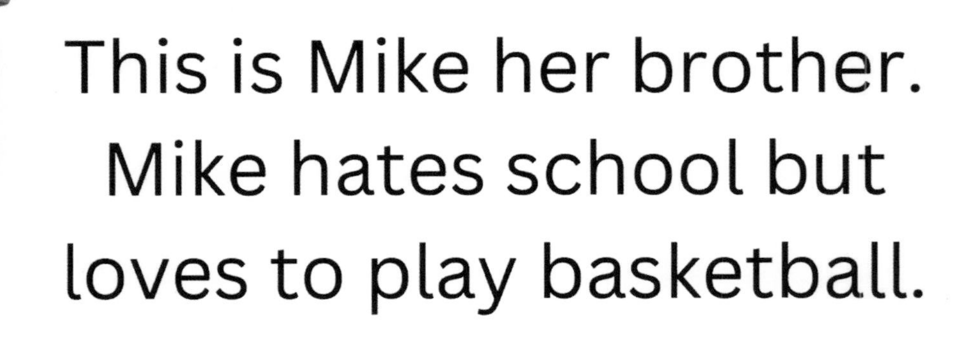

This is Mike her brother. Mike hates school but loves to play basketball.

Everyday Bella skips to school thinking of all the fun she will have.

12

The only thing Mike likes doing at school is playing on the basketball team.

When Bella gets to school she
meets her friend called Molly.

Molly is just like Bella. Molly loves
everything about school.

Their teacher is called Mr Millers. They love Mr Millers because he is fun.

Lessons for today:
Maths - 7, 8 & 9 times table
Reading
Have fun

Bella and Molly love learning in class, they have fun and giggle.

Bella and Molly both love maths. Their teacher Mr Millers makes learning fun.

They are learning their times tables today and Mr Millers makes it easier to learn by turning it in to a song for the class to sing.

At lunch time they love to go to the library and read.

When they are in the library they let their imaginations go wild.

Bella loves reading books about ballerinas and dreams of dancing on a big stage one day.

Molly loves to read about crystals, she loves how shiny and bright they are and how they sparkle in the sun light.

After school Bella and Molly practice playing their violins, they have entered in to the school talent show.

With the school talent show coming up soon, they practice playing their violins everyday after school.

They practice in Bella's bedroom and they are very loud. They play the same song over and over, wanting to get it just right.

5+4=9
9-5=?

Bella's brother Mike is trying to do his homework but he can't concentrate because the girls are being too noisy.

12

Mike decides to go out to play basketball instead.

Mike is very easily distracted. He will always prefer to play instead of doing his homework.

After finishing violin practice
Bella and Molly say goodbye.

They were really pleased with
how practice went and were
getting more excited about
performing at the talent show.

"Hmmmm I wonder what fun i'm going to have in school tomorrow....... I can't wait!!"

This book was written by Dillon Kirk-Harris with just a little help from her mum. Dillon is just 6 yrs old and this story has come straight from the imagination of Dillon herself.

Written by Dillon Kirk-Harris

Printed in Great Britain
by Amazon